PRAISE FOR N

A fabulous soaring thriller.

— *TAKE OVER AT MIDNIGHT,* MIDWEST
BOOK REVIEW

Meticulously researched, hard-hitting, and suspenseful.

— *PURE HEAT,* PUBLISHERS WEEKLY,
STARRED REVIEW

Expert technical details abound, as do realistic military missions with superb imagery that will have readers feeling as if they are right there in the midst and on the edges of their seats.

— *LIGHT UP THE NIGHT,* RT REVIEWS, 4
1/2 STARS

Buchman has catapulted his way to the top tier of my favorite authors.

— FRESH FICTION

Nonstop action that will keep readers on the edge of their seats.

— *TAKE OVER AT MIDNIGHT,* LIBRARY JOURNAL

M L. Buchman's ability to keep the reader right in the middle of the action is amazing.

— LONG AND SHORT REVIEWS

The only thing you'll ask yourself is, "When does the next one come out?"

— *WAIT UNTIL MIDNIGHT,* RT REVIEWS, 4 STARS

The first...of (a) stellar, long-running (military) romantic suspense series.

— *THE NIGHT IS MINE,* BOOKLIST, "THE 20 BEST ROMANTIC SUSPENSE NOVELS: MODERN MASTERPIECES"

I knew the books would be good, but I didn't realize how good.

— NIGHT STALKERS SERIES, KIRKUS REVIEWS

Buchman mixes adrenalin-spiking battles and brusque military jargon with a sensitive approach.

13 times "Top Pick of the Month"

Tom Clancy fans open to a strong female lead will clamor for more.

Superb! Miranda is utterly compelling!

Miranda Chase continues to astound and charm.

Escape Rating: A. Five Stars! OMG just start with *Drone* and be prepared for a fantastic binge-read!

The best military thriller I've read in a very long time. Love the female characters.

RETURN PASSAGE

A SAILING ROMANCE STORY

M. L. BUCHMAN

SIGN UP FOR M. L. BUCHMAN'S NEWSLETTER TODAY

and receive:
Release News
Free Short Stories
a Free Book

Get your free book today. Do it now.
free-book.mlbuchman.com

Other works by M. L. Buchman: (* - also in audio)

Action-Adventure Thrillers

Dead Chef
One Chef!
Two Chef!

Miranda Chase
Drone*
Thunderbolt*
Condor*
Ghostrider*
Raider*
Chinook*
Havoc*
White Top*
Start the Chase*

Science Fiction / Fantasy

Deities Anonymous
Cookbook from Hell: Reheated
Saviors 101

Single Titles
Monk's Maze
the Me and Elsie Chronicles

Contemporary Romance

Eagle Cove
Return to Eagle Cove
Recipe for Eagle Cove
Longing for Eagle Cove
Keepsake for Eagle Cove

Love Abroad
Heart of the Cotswolds: England
Path of Love: Cinque Terre, Italy

Where Dreams
Where Dreams are Born
Where Dreams Reside
Where Dreams Are of Christmas*
Where Dreams Unfold
Where Dreams Are Written
Where Dreams Continue

Non-Fiction

Strategies for Success
Managing Your Inner Artist/Writer
Estate Planning for Authors*
Character Voice
Narrate and Record Your Own
Audiobook*

Short Story Series by M. L. Buchman:

Action-Adventure Thrillers

Dead Chef

Miranda Chase Origin Stories

Romantic Suspense

Antarctic Ice Fliers

US Coast Guard

Contemporary Romance

Eagle Cove

Other

Deities Anonymous (fantasy)

Single Titles

The Emily Beale Universe
(military romantic suspense)

The Night Stalkers
MAIN FLIGHT
The Night Is Mine
I Own the Dawn
Wait Until Dark
Take Over at Midnight
Light Up the Night
Bring On the Dusk
By Break of Day
Target of the Heart
Target Lock on Love
Target of Mine
Target of One's Own
NIGHT STALKERS HOLIDAYS
Daniel's Christmas*
Frank's Independence Day*
Peter's Christmas*
Christmas at Steel Beach
Zachary's Christmas*
Roy's Independence Day*
Damien's Christmas*
Christmas at Peleliu Cove

Henderson's Ranch
Nathan's Big Sky*
Big Sky, Loyal Heart*
Big Sky Dog Whisperer*
Tales of Henderson's Ranch*

Shadow Force: Psi
At the Slightest Sound*
At the Quietest Word*
At the Merest Glance*
At the Clearest Sensation*

White House Protection Force
Off the Leash*
On Your Mark*
In the Weeds*

Firehawks
Pure Heat
Full Blaze
Hot Point*
Flash of Fire*
Wild Fire
SMOKEJUMPERS
Wildfire at Dawn*
Wildfire at Larch Creek*
Wildfire on the Skagit*

Delta Force
Target Engaged*
Heart Strike*
Wild Justice*
Midnight Trust*

Emily Beale Universe Short Story Series
The Night Stalkers
The Night Stalkers Stories
The Night Stalkers CSAR
The Night Stalkers Wedding Stories
The Future Night Stalkers

Delta Force
Th Delta Force Shooters
The Delta Force Warriors

Firehawks
The Firehawks Lookouts
The Firehawks Hotshots
The Firebirds

White House Protection Force
Stories

Future Night Stalkers
Stories (Science Fiction)

ABOUT THIS BOOK

A musician seeks inspiration on the open sea
and finds it in the most unexpected way.

MYLES AND ROSE ARE TWINS. DESPITE THE SUCCESS OF their musical duet, they can't manage to break out. Myles knows they're missing something if only he could pin it down.

Vonda's attempts to restart her life keep sinking beneath the waves. She needs to chart a new course.

A chance meeting on Maui and a leisurely five-week sailboat ride to Victoria, Canada changes the future for all three of them.

1

THE HULL CREAKED AS THE SUBMARINE *ATLANTIS* SLIPPED beneath the waves. They sat in sideways-facing seats made of plastic darker blue than the ocean depths. In front of each seat were big round portholes to observe the Hawaiian reefs in all of their glorious color. Sunbeams struck down through crystal blue waters as if they'd entered a particularly soothing space warp.

Forty tourists sat in two out-facing rows down the length of the single cabin. The two pilots and the guide were perched up at the bow.

"Wild!" Rose whispered from behind him. They'd chosen back-to-back seats in the twenty-meter-long submarine so that, between them, they wouldn't miss anything.

But Myles Lauer was too busy listening to the music of it to notice much else. The sub made a hell of song descending to cruise the reefs off western Maui.

Ping. Ping, Creak. The hull set an atmosphere of tension as the water pressure compressed the hull. Not loud enough to be unnerving, but it let him know they were entering another world. How to translate that into a song?

Welcome to somewhere you've never been before.

He'd often couldn't pin down the answers, but he liked to keep feeding his subconscious ideas to play with.

The tour guide spoke with that lazy lilt of Hawaii that always made life sound so much fun. Little dabs of pidgin only added to the rhythm and the feeling.

"Check it out, you folks on the starboard. See dat eel under the blue coral fan giving us the stink eye? He be a real moke, you go divin', you don't want to screw with him. On the port, remember that's the left side, see the blacktip reef shark? He's brown with black tips on his fins. He's truly a sweetheart. Five feet, this is a big one. Lives on little fishes and maybe crabs. He no mess with you if you no mess with him."

The sunlight shifted, fading only a little as the forty-five-minute tour took them deeper. But that was Rose's thing. She saw colors in ways he couldn't imagine. She's the one who brought the harmonies to their music.

New melodies always surrounded Myles at every turn, like how the schools of fish swirled by the porthole glass. A small cluster of black-and-white-striped Moorish Idols with splashes of sunshine yellow that looked like someone had spilled the final color over parts their white by accident. A refrain so predictable that everyone's ready to sing along, hit with a splash of Rose's harmony? Maybe a twist in the final line of each repeat. *Yeah, like that.*

A school of purple triggerfish swirled by like a high riff, scattering from the plodding bass of a solo green sea turtle, lazing over the reef. The coral offered up accent notes in orange, white, blue, gold. Sprays of fantastical fans rose above the stable touchstone backbeat of the globular brain coral.

He barely noticed the supposed highlight of the dive. The sub company had sunk an aged steel replica of an even older wooden schooner that had been a whaling museum for years. The original had actually spent its working life as a trade ship until it was cast in the whaling role for Michener's *Hawaii*. Now its replica was an artificial reef with fifteen years of growth on it. Bottom line, it wasn't as old as it looked. Fish and coral grew on it. No rousing through-line of story or rollicking chorus, at least not one that he could find.

As the sub circled at its lazy walking pace to reveal the ship to the passengers on the other side, he stared out across the sandy plain. Maybe Rose would see something in the wreck that he didn't. In the midst of the busy emptiness there was a sudden disturbance. A ray flapped up out of the sand, creating a cloud of fine grit in the water, then breaking free of the cloud like a sailboat emerging from a squall line.

Revealed, it had three-meter-wide wings of black covered in white polka dots. The beat of its wings were as slow and lazy as the turtle's. Too slow. Myles wanted up-tempo. He wanted energy. Yet that rippling wingbeat rang clear as a pulse in his head.

Their duo made their money in playing bar gigs. Packing the dance floors all over Seattle from the Tractor Tavern to the J&M had made them popular, but they couldn't find the next level. They should be playing Q

Nightclub or Supernova Seattle. At Bumbershoot they never got near the main stages unless they were down front with the other dancers. And national tours? They'd only done one of the Western Washington county fairs.

"That pod of pilot whales was so cool," Rose spoke as they filed out of the sub, climbing to the deck, and crossing over to the waiting speedboat to return them to the harbor.

"What whales?" He actually didn't remember anything much since watching that ray rise up out of the sand. There must be something there, but the beat was odd.

"That pod that circled the sub three times wondering if the sub was a new kind of whale."

Myles looked down at the water off the side as Rose laughed at him. Nothing to see despite the clear water. He shrugged at her. His twin sister always knew that he got lost in his head.

2

The Dirty Monkey was prime dancing turf in Lahaina.

They'd pre-arranged to play a three-night series here before they'd flown from Seattle to Maui. This trip was a creative break, but playing a gig also gave them an excuse to write it off on their taxes. In truth, the two-month break was because Myles was going insane going nowhere—career limbo.

Time for something completely different.

Two weeks kicking around the Maui paradise and then ferry a sailboat back to Victoria, British Columbia. The annual Vic-Maui Yacht Race had left BC for the two-week hustle down the trade winds to Lahaina Harbor at about the same time he and Rose had stepped on a plane in Seattle. There'd be a hell of a party after the race, and then volunteer return crews would board the boats to sail them back, while the owners and race crews hopped their flights home.

For the return crews it was a long slow ride north to catch the Japanese Current and slide across then down to

Victoria Harbor. A five-week luxury ride they'd done seven times over the years. The first time had been between junior and senior year of high school for their next-door neighbor. No need to own a boat, just deliver it home in one piece. Sweet!

They wrote a lot of music on those long rides, yet another argument for the tax man on why it should be a write-off.

The Dirty Monkey was anything but. It was in the heart of Lahaina and the bar filled the second floor of a Front Street building. Big windows opened onto a balcony overlooking the narrow two-lane with wide sidewalks. It was a walking kind of town, for both tourists and locals. Hopefully that meant it was a dancing kind of town.

It had none of the funk feel of most of the places they usually played. The fake white marble bar was surrounded by steel stools. The floor had high-top tables that could seat six, or a dozen crowded around if they were standing. Behind the bar was a wide selection of beer taps and bottled liquor. Especially whiskey—they had lots of that.

Their wood floor showed heavy wear, the kind that came from a serious amount of dancing. Tonight VMR's music would be pumping out the windows.

He and Rose had named their band for *Very Myles and Rose.* Or maybe *Very Much Reality!* Or... They kept thinking up new acronyms—they couldn't even settle on their name, never mind what brand would make their careers really take off.

Myles had loved the energy of performing since he

was born, at least that's how Dad told it. Every time he said it, Mom would rub her belly as if it hurt, *Started way before birth, honey!* Myles had dragged his much shyer twin sister along for the ride.

It had all sorts of advantages beyond how their music fit together.

They received so many compliments from strangers on what a good-looking couple they were, that they'd stopped correcting people except when it mattered.

They couldn't have looked much more different and still had the same parents. But at their senior prom he'd won Handsomest Prince to stand beside Beautifulest Princess. Neither of their dates had been surprised or much begrudged them that. He'd taken after Dad's fair and blond. Big sister Rose, all of eleven minutes older, had Mom's darker coloring and long mahogany hair framing a narrow face. Both five-eleven, they looked like blond and brown bookends.

Another advantage was when he was about to do something stupid with a girl, Rose could snag his elbow with a, *Come along, dear.* If she had a guy she couldn't shed, Myles would walk off with her hand-in-hand.

They had a mutual support pact that had seen each through a lot of challenging times.

And the music. Myles knew they were good. The penny had dropped, dime, nickel, and quarter too. But the silver dollar wouldn't fall. They made a living, but it was a good thing they shared an apartment and preferred a pub meal to a steak house for the rare meal out.

He pulled out his travel guitar. Little more than the fretboard and bridge carved out of maple with the tuning machines tucked into the small body of the instrument, it weighed three pounds and fit in the overhead bin on an airplane. Hell, it was small enough, he could plug in headphones and *play* on an airplane without disturbing anyone.

Rose slung on her traveling bass, all of six inches longer. They plugged into the bar's sound system and began to play.

They'd had a lot of trial and error on what worked and what didn't. Originally they'd warm up the crowd with a few mellow songs, get the audience used to the shift to live music, then hit them with a dance beat.

Not anymore. It was early yet, but fifteen people in a bar that could hold a hundred was a thin crowd. Still...

Myles double-checked that the doors over the street were open, and nodded for Rose to punch into one of their hotter dance riffs. It was a long thing with no words. Rose had found an irresistible heavy beat and he'd built a playful melody onto it, like a cat chasing a windup mouse. Even in an audience of two, it set people dancing.

By the time they finished it, half the bar was dancing, which was now more like forty people. The owner was too busy with drink orders to even shoot them a smile, exactly the way he'd want to be.

It was deep in their second set when he noticed her—dramatic as hell.

It wasn't her height, a leggy five-eight. Or her crazy Hawaiian head scarf that covered her hair, including her eyebrows, like she was a woman of mystery. In the dim light of the evening, there was no way to tell anything about much about her build. Slender, maybe, and far enough to the back that she kept disappearing from view.

Still, she was incredible to watch.

Her dance moves weren't star-dancer amazing, but her timing was out of this world.

With her body, she wove a counterpoint around Myles' own melody as if he were the one playing the supporting bassline. He shifted the next verse and she wove back to his original melody as if teasing him for abandoning it. Rose looked at him, Myles could feel it, but he stayed focused on the dancer.

Not really watching the stage or her own place in the crowd, she and Myles played a game anyway. Her knee would find Rose's backbeat, picking out that F-sharp three-below-middle-C every time the bass ventured there. He'd written this number in G-major with a I-V-vi-IV—G, D, E-minor, C—chord progression as a tongue-in-cheek homage to the *most overused sensitive female progression* in pop music.

Then the woman's elbow would pick up the low E but on an off-rhythm accented by a head shaking G. When he moved to match, she slid into Rose's low C with a two-footed thump, and then started building again. Rose slid underneath their melody and harmony like she was laying down the world's oceans for their hull and sails to best ride on.

Between the three of them, they built the night layer upon layer. No more set breaks. The floor packed tighter than a mosh pit. At one point the bartenders were up and dancing on the bar top.

When the end came, it wasn't planned or

orchestrated, it was simply the final note of how the night fit together. They returned to that first dance instrumental, but embellished and built in ways that reflected their three-way dance to the music.

By the last chord, the crowd was exhausted, ecstatic, and dancing each to their own beats of music as they stormed the bar.

That's when he made his mistake and glanced at Rose. They grinned at each other like two lost fools.

By the time he turned back, the scarfed dancer was gone.

3

"I swear to God she was real," Myles knew he was repeating himself pointlessly. His voice died flat against the cave's walls.

"God, Myles, drop it."

For a change of pace to their last day on Hawaii, they'd rented scooters and were circling Maui. Rose had turned at the sign for the Hana Lava Tube and now they were inside it and it was eating his sound. The entry fee included a flashlight and there were self-guided tour signs along the way.

He tended to breeze by those and then plague Rose to tell him the story as she read each one to the last comma and period. She was countering that by reading halfway, laughing at something, then finishing and walking away without a word. Which meant he'd have to read it himself —and it *was* interesting. By the third or fourth sign, he was skimming them for himself, then his sister would laugh and he'd have to backtrack to figure out why. She was right of course.

The lava that had formed this tube a thousand years ago had layered thickly over the top. Most of the ceiling was sixty feet or more thick and topped with soil and tropical growth madness outside.

After entering through a narrow opening and descending a flight of stairs, they were soon in the quarter-mile long tube. Big enough that even claustrophobes wouldn't have an issue and long enough that the other people there didn't make it feel crowded.

Part of that was because the wall ate up all of the sound. No long echoes in the Hana Lava Tube. Inside the vast tube, their voices were strangely dead. Whispers didn't carry five feet. He felt as if he had to shout a little to hear his own voice at all.

"It's the rock," Rose had always paid more attention in science class than he had. "It's so porous that the sound gets lost in it like commercial baffling."

"Fine. I'll use some to build our next sound booth." They had a small three-bedroom apartment and the third room had been lined with old quilts they'd picked up at garage sales. It made for a colorful recording studio. Too bad that neither of them were yet satisfied with the music they were producing so that they could release any of it.

"Do that!" Rose snapped, clearly sick of him. She had a point, he was fairly sick of himself. Starting tomorrow they'd be out on the sea. There he could just chill and fall into the routines of sailing, eating, and sleeping. If they caught a storm, they caught one, but there wasn't any heavy weather predicted. If they didn't he'd write music.

They'd sung two more nights at The Dirty Monkey, packed 'em in tight. But they'd never hit the deep groove again. It was like he'd been offered a peek of that next-level sound, his nose pressed to the proverbial window as he hung onto the ledge by his very fingernails.

But he couldn't sustain it and was once again mortal. And the fall hurt as assuredly as if it had been physical.

A good crowd but not all dancing. A happy owner, the first night's success had spread by word of mouth, but the next night there were almost as many drinking as there were dancing. No bartenders dancing on the marble bar top.

Not without...*her.*

"She wasn't a phantom or a phantasm or a poltergeist or imaginary or any of that."

Rose's look said he'd crossed over that edge where his sister always shifted into neutral mode. She wasn't going to react to or offer anything until he chilled. They both agreed that she'd laid down the hottest bass lines of her life, but she insisted that she'd only been taking her cues from him—if that didn't beat all.

"Maybe you were seeing her subconsciously..." Because if she had been, then the mystery dancer had indeed been real.

Rose's look told him that she'd been following his lead and he was badly overreaching. But if he had been imagining the dancer, then why hadn't he been able to find the music again on subsequent nights.

"Fine. I'll just focus on the lava tube."

"Finally," Rose's tone was rich with disbelief that it might last longer than any other subject had from the last three days.

Not another word. He wouldn't bring up the mystery dancer—now MD in his thoughts—ever again.

Besides, it was their last day on Maui. The Vic-Maui sailboats were in, the big finisher's party was tonight. Tomorrow, they'd meet the skipper for the handoff to the return crews and they'd be out on the high seas. Giving up on Lahaina, they were cruising the hundred-mile loop around the island. His chances of meeting MD the mystery dancer ever again were diminishing by the minute.

And the lava tube *was* interesting. The surfaces kept changing. One area was all sharp ʻaʻā. It prickled his palm when he touched it, and it gulped up the sound of a tongue-click or finger-snap like a dog eating steak. Pāhoehoe layered over other surfaces in smooth twisty ropes. One chamber was thick with the stuff, like someone had poured milk chocolate on all the walls and ceiling. Sound didn't disappear on this texture. In fact, he kept catching licks and hints of the music they'd played that first night.

Not in his voice. Not in Rose's smooth alto. But—

And it was gone before he could ask if Rose heard it. Just a cluster of notes, flitting through his messed-up brain probably created because he wanted that next whatever-it-was so badly.

It was agony to have created, but to no longer quite able to hear what he'd done.

Because he hadn't done it alone.

Not even with Rose.

It was—right back where he started—MD.

He was blinking hard at the daylight as they emerged

from the cool depths back into the heat of the day. Again, he'd missed whole portions of the adventure as he'd tried to grab onto those lost melodies that haunted him.

The heat and humidity were a hard slap after an hour underground. Mid-July was actually a crap time to be hanging out on Maui, but it wasn't his call when the Vic-Maui ran. It wasn't like Florida hideous, but it was more than his Seattle blood was used to.

"Let's head back."

Rose didn't point out that they were already doing that, having gone two-thirds around the island. She also was kind enough to not point out that he wasn't going to find MD.

4

VONDA DECOSTA EMERGED FROM THE RED TI BOTANICAL Garden Maze, slightly dizzy from the constant direction changes, not that it was that hard a maze. Her metabolism was *so* screwed up.

The lava tube had been cool, but she'd been all goosebumps and wishing for a parka by the end of the underground walk. Humming to distract herself had helped...a little. A leisurely walk in the sun-saturated hedge maze had been what the doctor ordered—with a few less turns. She cleared her head with a final shake.

Doctor ordered! There was a phrase she could finally purge from her soul—fingers and toes crossed.

At the southern edge of the park that included the Hana Lava Tube, they'd built a maze out of red ti trees. They had big, lush-red leaves as long as her forearm that grew as thickly as a hedge. Shaped into a solid wall from knee-high to several feet over her head, they defined the passages but let the sun pour down.

As she'd wandered the paths, ignoring the little map,

not caring if she dead-ended here or retraced her steps there, she played with the music.

She'd forgotten how much she'd missed the music of her college *a cappella* days until it had reached out through the open windows of The Dirty Monkey and dragged her off the street. For the first time in a year, she'd stopped thinking, stopped worrying. For the first time in the years since college, she'd simply given herself up to the music.

And way the hell overdone it.

Jesus, Vonda! You gotta be more careful.

She was supposed to be over all this. Three months of chemo. Two-to-one recovery time meant six more months of climbing out of the hole that the chemicals and radiation had driven her into. She'd done all that and yet felt completely strung out from a single night of dancing.

How long are you gonna wallow?

A week ago, she'd have answered, *forever.*

The disease.

Then quitting her job to focus on her wellness.

Next her fiancé hadn't been able to deal with the future of a woman in her twenties who'd already had stage-two cancer. He'd kept emphasizing the *two* until she'd have probably thrown him out if he hadn't already left.

Now, as clean as they could test six months after end of treatment.

None of that had mattered. He'd been gone while she'd been still shaking from the second dose of chemo.

To hell with him and to hell with her past.

If the disease hadn't been what exhausted her, perhaps it was that she hadn't rebuilt her stamina at all.

Yet exhausting herself past reason wasn't the only thing that had happened that night.

Sure, she'd slept hard most of the day after that dance, but it hadn't been mere exhaustion or the muscles so unused to the workout. She'd been caught in the trap for a year: diagnosis, second opinions, treatment, and recovery. Somehow, in that one blissful, passed-out sleep, she'd walked out the other side of the trap and left it behind.

Vonda knew about the *now,* right down deep in a way no always-healthy person could know. The time to make choices and changes was right now. It was *always* right now. Learn and grow. The dance had heaved overboard all that crap past; poor-ass choice of fiancé included.

Head scarves? Done!

She tugged it off her head and ran her fingers through the three inches of dark-blonde that had finally grown out. The warm breeze washing over the botanic garden with all of its foreign tropical sweetness caressed her scalp anew. Maybe she'd get some mousse and spike it. Dye it purple? Wouldn't *that* put her parents in a twist? Actually, Mom would probably go to the salon with her and get a color to match.

Christ but she'd be dead without them. Last thing they needed was their grown daughter re-intruding on their lives, but they'd been there for her every step of the way. Mom sympathized and coddled her. Dad didn't say much, but had become her go-to for wheels when she had the hundred-thousandth doctor's appointment. He was also the one who'd suggested she go to Hawaii for a break to celebrate the *supposed* end of recovery. Did it in his normally voluble way of slipping a plane ticket across the dinner table. Without a word, of course, but he did it.

Kicking me out? Vonda had asked.

Mom had made consoling sounds, as surprised as she was. Dad had shrugged a maybe. Not that he wanted her gone, but maybe that it was time.

And he'd been right. It was time to do things new and different.

She'd been here long enough to find her favorite beach. And yesterday, after sleeping away the day before, she'd spent bodysurfing on Slaughterhouse Beach up the coast. Backed by a steep cliff, and fronted by a snorkeling reef where she'd teased clown fish and carefully avoided a giant green sea turtle, she'd soaked up sun on the sand and cooled off under the trees. Such a blessing to be outdoors.

Today she was touring the sections of the island she hadn't seen in her three weeks here. Time to stretch herself.

Tomorrow? Who knew.

As she crossed from the maze back to the parking lot, she saw the two musicians from The Dirty Monkey heading there from the lava tube. She'd slept through their second show and been too enamored of the sunset on Slaughterhouse Beach to go to the third.

They were already on their scooters and tugging on helmets. She wanted to thank them, but it would sound stupid. Too...she didn't know what.

But as her feet remained rooted to the spot and they

started their engines with a quick little splutter, she knew that was the old her. The one who had become so fragile that all action was terrifying.

"Hey! Wait!" The man pulled away without hearing, but the woman turned to look in her direction. She couldn't remember their names. She hadn't even looked at the poster by the door. Vonda had been walking the street looking for somewhere to have dinner and ended up on the dance floor with no conscious transition.

"Hey, yourself." The woman looked so amazing, all tall and elegant. Her shining hair far longer than Vonda had ever grown her own. All of the things that Vonda wasn't.

"You two were amazing the other night!" She blurted it out like a total fan girl.

"Thanks," the woman smiled. It wasn't something she'd done very often that night. At the bar she'd been the consummate chill bass player, cool and sexy beyond words or music.

"I missed the last two nights. When are you playing again?" Because she was so ready to shed more of her past.

The smile faded. "Six weeks until our next gig, sorry."

"Oh," she could feel her own smile die. Six weeks? Would she still be here then? Probably not. She'd been in day-to-day mode, but there was an energy now. A desire to move ahead. Except she wasn't sure what that meant anymore. Back to her old job? Legal secretary had paid the bills, but she didn't exactly miss it—like at all!

"If you're in Seattle, we'll be at a place called the High Dive."

"Oh! I live in Seattle."

The woman looked down the road after her lover, husband, whatever. Their deep connection on stage had been unmistakable. "Maybe we'll see you then."

"Six weeks," it sounded so long. "Nowhere sooner?"

"We'll be at sea on the Vic-Maui Return for the next five weeks. The only place we'll be playing is on the sailboat."

It had been impossible to miss the mayhem that had hit Lahaina. A banner year, twenty-three yachts had completed the long race. Two more were still expected, after the time limit had expired but in time for tonight's party. Three more had retired and dropped out. Several hundred sailing crew had hit the small town of Lahaina as if they'd been at sea for two years not two weeks.

"You're sailing back to Victoria for five weeks?" Vonda couldn't imagine what that would be like.

"Sure. We've done it several times."

And it was one of *those* moments.

Vonda felt herself rising up on her toes as if to resist falling forward from a gentle nudge behind. Taking the next step after Greg had walked out on her. Getting on the plane to Hawaii. Going...

One of those moments she'd so often dodged in the past.

The past.

Done with wallowing, huh?

She opened her eyes and looked at the woman.

Vonda still didn't know her name.

It didn't matter.

The wind was blowing from behind her. She'd sailed

before. Never on one of the big boats like the line of forty- and fifty-footers presently anchored off Lahaina's shore. But she'd sailed. That had to count for something, didn't it?

"Need another hand? I've sailed in smaller boats."

"It's four or five weeks. And there can be some bad storms."

"Don't care." Even if there was no music, no dancing. "If there's no room on yours, how about another boat? How do I find out? I mean—"

The woman's smile cut her off.

Vonda bit her tongue and tried to chill. Something she'd never been particularly good at...before the cancer. It was actually kind of neat that the excitement had come back. Until now she'd wondered if she'd ever be excited about something again.

"I'll ask around. Meet us for breakfast tomorrow at seven in the 808 Grindz Cafe?"

"Sure. I like that place." She'd actually eaten her way through most of the menu and put on some much-needed weight as she'd inhaled a three-egg omelet with fried spam, corned beef hash, and ham fried rice on successive mornings. She rarely needed lunch after one of their breakfasts, but the place was addictive.

"Okay, I'd better go catch up with Myles. He'll eventually notice I'm missing. I don't want him thinking I'm dead on the road." And she motored off.

"Thanks!" Vonda thought to shout too little too late. But the woman, whose name she still didn't know, raised a hand in a wave and raced out of the parking lot. At least raced as fast as an island scooter could go.

Vonda repeated Myles' name a few time to be sure to remember it.

"Well now you've done it, Vonda," she said to no one at all.

She had.

"No commitments needed until you step on the boat."

Too late. She was so there already.

5

SEVEN A.M. AT THE 808 GRINDZ?

Vonda was there at six with her backpack beside her. By six-thirty she'd turned a Mowie Wowie omelet into a thousand tiny egg cubes on her plate, her hot cocoa was cold, and her pineapple juice warm.

At six-fifty, a big guy in his fifties came in, and scanned the diners. His eyes locked on her and he headed straight over to her sitting alone at a table for four.

Oh shit!

She checked around. The place was busy enough that he wouldn't try anything here. But she'd have to leave to get away from him. Then he might follow. And Vonda would miss the musicians. And—

"You the one wants to sail the return?"

The relief and disappointment warred within her. He wasn't a threat, but it meant she'd be on a different boat than the musicians. Vonda managed a weak nod.

He sat down across from her without asking. Would

she feel safe on this guy's boat? What if it was just them? She didn't like the sound of that at all.

"Why should I let you on my boat?" He flagged down a waitress for a cup of coffee.

His arrogance ticked her off. He reminded him too much of her fiancé...ex-fiancé. "Why should *I* want to go on *your* boat? Plenty to choose from."

His smile was fast. "Most of the crews are already set. You're running out of choices."

Crap! She'd barely slept throughout the night, instead imaging sailing out of the past she'd been mired in. And now the life had gone out of it.

"Are you spooking my new friend, Barry?" The musician woman slid into one of the open seats.

"Nah, Rose. Just trying to find out if she's a good one or if you'll have to dump her overboard after the first hundred miles."

Vonda couldn't suppress the squeak of fear that being set adrift in the middle of the ocean evoked.

"Your sense of humor is one of the reasons we're glad you're flying home this afternoon." Rose said in her quiet steady way.

Breathe, Vonda reminded herself. *Just breathe.*

Barry rolled his eyes. "Just having a bit of fun. Seriously though," he didn't look any more or less serious as he turned back to face Vonda, "what *are* your qualifications?"

Vonda tried to come up with some, but couldn't. "Absolutely none. The biggest boat I've ever been on was a Cal 23, cruising on Lake Washington."

"Cruising? More like wallowing on a fat rubber ducky

in a bathtub! Long damn way from my J/160." Barry looked aside, "This is the one you want to take deep sea, Rose?"

Vonda quickly repeated Rose a few times. Myles and Rose. Myles and Rose.

Rose shrugged. "She asked. I like her."

Barry looked back and forth between them, then finally nodded. "Your call. There's enough foul weather gear aboard to take care of her. The return isn't my ride, just my boat. So don't break her on the way home." He slugged back the rest of his still-steaming coffee like it was a shot of tequila, pushed back, and tipped his head toward Vonda. "Might be nice for my liability insurance if you don't break the girl either."

A silence settled over the table after he was gone. Rose waited long enough for the jumble of Vonda's thoughts to settle.

"Me? You like me? But you don't know me." Not that she knew Myles or Rose either.

"Do I need a reason?" Rose's smile was easy to return.

"Not if it gets me on the boat."

6

Her afternoons on Margo's Cal 23 puttering around Lake Washington did nothing at all to prepare her for the *Maybelline.* Six people could fit in the cockpit of Margo's little twenty-three-footer, hip-to-shoulder and bumping knees.

The *Maybelline* was an awe-inspiring fifty-three feet long and fifteen wide. The mast towered forever above her head. The cockpit was filled with a bewildering array of lines, winches, and a steering wheel so big that there was a notch in the deck for the lower part to swing in. But eight could still sit on the cushioned seats, not counting the person behind the wheel.

"How many people are needed to sail it?" she asked Rose.

"To sail *her?* Two can manage for a cruise. On the race down, she had a crew of ten. Helmsman, navigator, two winchmen, and a foredeck hand. Two watches."

Vonda's unintended glance at her bare wrist earned

Rose's soft laugh. Vonda knew what it meant and struggled not to feel foolish as Rose explained.

"A watch is a shift. But on a boat like this that's a loose term. One of us can handle the boat in most conditions, two if it gets nasty. All ten if you're racing hot in a strong blow, whether or not it's your time to sleep."

"There are going to be ten of us?" It was a big boat, but that would be a bigger crowd than she'd hung out with in a long time.

"Three. You're the third. We'll up-anchor as soon as Myles gets here with the rest of the groceries." Myles, Myles, she repeated a few more times. His name had become a mantra of hope somewhere in the long night. Myles and Rose.

Vonda hadn't thought about the food. Five weeks' worth for her to be aboard. "I can pay for—"

Rose waved it away. "Barry pays for it. It's traditional. Most boat return crews are unpaid, but the owner covers all expenses to have his boat sailed home. You get the forward cabin. Go ahead and stow your gear. I'll scrounge slicks, a float jacket, and a life preserver for you before we go."

"Like a kid?"

"Underway, we'll all wear them except in the calmest weather *and* we're all three awake. You'll get used to it." Rose waved her below.

Vonda descended the ladder into the main cabin and could only gawk.

Margo's Cal 23 had two tiny bunks that were buried under rubber bumpers used at dock, a scattering of lines, and a cooler of beer squashed in among the raincoats.

The *Maybelline* was finished throughout in lustrous wood planking like...she didn't know what...a sailboat? To her left was an efficient kitchen that would be perfect for a luxury studio apartment. A top-opening fridge and freezer were set into the countertop. It had a sink, lots of cupboards, even a small stove and oven. It swung lightly back and forth with the rocking of the boat. She gave it a poke and it swung more. Oh, for when the boat was heeled over, it would stay level. Neat!

To her right was a seat with a table surrounded by more radios and navigation gear than she'd ever imagined. The table was like those old school desks with the lift-up lid. She peeked and it held logbooks and charts, presumably if the equipment broke down. In a drawer she found a steel sextant. That made her feel a little safer, though she had no idea how to use one. An instruction book was tucked in beside it and Vonda vowed to learn that skill before they reached Seattle.

As she moved forward, there were big comfortable bench seats to either side, long enough to stretch out on, and a folded-up table in the middle of the aisle. With the flaps raised, it could seat at least six or seven comfortably.

Beyond that was a grand master suite—at least grand in a very small-space way. A bed big enough for two on the left. Closet and dresser on the right. Straight ahead a shower and sink, and a toilet with enough levers to run a spaceship. She'd definitely need lessons on that. There was a big round metal pole by the door that she finally realized was the bottom of the mast that passed through the floor as well.

But this couldn't be right. Rose and Myles must sleep here, yet there were no clothes or personal stuff.

She set her pack down on the deck and returned aft to ask what she was missing.

As she returned, she saw what it was for herself.

Because she'd been facing forward, she'd missed that to either side of the ladder descending from the cockpit, toward the rear, were two more suites. Each had a bed as big as the one up forward. Oddly, there was gear stowed in both of those rather than all in one.

She also found a second bathroom behind a closed door. Well, maybe the forward suite actually was hers, far more luxury than she'd expected. Vonda had imagined a bigger version of Margo's plastic-coated bench seats in a cramped cabin.

This boat she could happily move aboard and never leave.

"Here, catch!" A male voice called. She turned barely in time to catch a bag with three big loaves of fresh-baked bread.

That was how she met Myles Lauer.

_____

7

"ARE WE RACING?" VONDA ASKED IN BREATHY EXCITEMENT.

Somewhere around the time they graduated from cradles to cribs, Myles had learned to trust Rose's judgement of people. So, he wasn't worried about Vonda Decosta, but he didn't know quite what to make of her either.

She was cute, pleasant, and her arms and legs were about as big around as pencils. But a joy radiated from the woman that made the sun shine brighter off the tropical water and the greens of Maui hillsides beckon deeper and richer.

He always spent too much time worrying, and Vonda brought none of that. She appeared to be a carefree sprite on the verge of hyperventilating with her passion. And she was being damned cute in the process.

"Not real racing," Rose answered before he could. "A lot of the return boats depart at the same time. Think of it as a casual race but mostly it's safety in numbers if anyone gets in trouble. We'll spread out over time, but probably never more than a day or so apart. Though we could well be in the lead most of the way, *Maybelline* is the largest and one of the fastest boats this year."

Myles tried to remember the last time Rose had said as many words in a row. He couldn't.

As he had the helm at the moment, Rose led Vonda around the boat, preparing for departure. They were anchored offshore in the Lahaina Roads, but the boat had been wrapped up tight during the week since its arrival.

Rose demonstrated how to prep the lines and then the two of them began unwrapping the sails. When they were ready, he raised the main and heaved it in close. That kept *Maybelline's* bow into the wind.

Then they set the big forward genoa, but left it to slap in the breeze.

Rose made quick work of heaving the anchor aboard, securing it, and making sure all of the rode, both chain and line, were fed cleanly into the chain locker.

He could see that Vonda was game, but she was even weaker than her thin limbs made her look. Oh well, she could still help with chores and cooking. Keep a soul company on those long silent watches.

At least she wasn't a chatterer.

While they secured the anchor, he spun the wheel to starboard. *Maybelline* drifted backward and twisted as she came off the anchor and the sails took the wind. They lost less than a boat length before there were moving forward. He spun the wheel to center, hauled in on the gennie sheet, and they were eased ahead smoothly.

A casual glance around showed he wasn't first off the anchor...but he was close. And because the others were to the south, he was first on the northern tack up the Roads, the channel between Maui and Molokai.

He didn't much care, but Barry had been at the dock to see him off. *Give 'em hell, Myles.* He'd bet that Barry was watching from the shore and grinning as they pulled away first. The man was competitive in ways Myles would never understand.

His body remembered as much as he did himself. As the sails drew, the boat began to put on way, he was already coiling lines properly to set for the next tack— though with these perfect winds, that could be hundreds of miles ahead.

As he worked in the cockpit while Rose and Vonda finished on the deck, he felt the music of the waves wash over him. It had been far too long since he'd sailed. Barry had missed last year's race with a fractured keel, and it had been too late to arrange a ride with anyone else.

Once they were cleaned up and solidly underway, he made a strumming motion to signal Rose to grab his guitar. *Maybelline* had settled into her course like a prime mare out for a lazy canter, loping over the waves with little tending needed. He set the autopilot and watched for a minute to make sure it was behaving.

He took the small travel guitar, plugged in a book-sized powered-speaker, and gave it a strum to check the tuning as he rested a foot on one of the lower wheel spokes so that he could keep track of what the autopilot was up to.

Myles fooled around with a few minor chords, but it wasn't a minor chord sort of day. C? No, the slightly deeper G, they were on an ocean, not a lake.

Vonda dropped an iced tea in the holder by the wheel for him, and then stretched out on a cockpit seat as if she'd never been anywhere else. That smile of purest joy was plastered on her face.

He futzed around with a few chords, but decided to keep it simple. It was that sort of a ride on the waves today.

"*Sailing it's...*" he started out then spotted the look of bliss on Vonda's face, "*Such a joy.*" He tried the line a few times with different cord progressions. Nope, keep it simple: G, C.

"*Sailing it's such a joy...*" he repeated it a few times. First with a folk strum, then he tried picking some of the notes, and finally settled on an upbeat sea chanty strum.

"*Sailing it's such a joy.*" The autopilot briefly lifted, then lowered his foot on the wheel spoke. Like he was playing in a bathtub. "*Sailboat just a big kid's toy.*" Barry was definitely a big kid when it came to the subject of his sailboat.

Myles tweaked the autopilot heading as they cleared the Lahaina Roads and headed north into the open sea. Rose ran out the main and gennie for best draw on the new heading.

"*Sailing along that reach,*" a glance behind, "*Anchor right off the big gold beach.*"

He backtracked through the two lines as Rose brought out her bass and a small speaker of her own. He was running G, C, D, G...but that felt like a verse, not a chorus.

Rose thumped out a G, C, G, D. Rocking the chords with the rhythm of the boat. Absolutely right.

Sippin' wine with the settin' sun,
Stars coming out, look I see first one!
(He always loved the first night at sea.)
Sailing's just right for me.
I'm just a natural born sailor, can't you see!

He rocked the melody back and forth a few times as Rose came in under him to set it solid and ocean deep.

A verse. Hmm... He eyed Vonda. Clearly a neophyte.

First time I ever sailed a boat,
Could hardly believe I was afloat,
Sailed upon a little lake,
(Rose had told him about her sole experience on Lake Washington.)
Oops! Watch that sail, feel the sun bake.
Was a time of so much joy,
Back when I was jes' a little-bitty (girl didn't fit, so he put in himself) *boy.*

All morning they fooled with verses. He sang a sailor's lifetime of verses. Spinning out different versions until they merged and blurred.

When finally his fingers were sore and his stomach was growling, he put aside the guitar.

"Damn I wish I'd recorded some of that."

Vonda handed him a notebook and a pen with a well-chewed end.

And there it was.

Three verses and a tight chorus. The first verse hadn't changed much, all about the joy of sailing. The second verse of adventures. Good lines that Vonda had mixed and matched. He'd never put them together this way, but there the adventures were: dolphins off the bow, the small port towns, and the new friends that always floated there.

The third verse was years later. Not some romantic ending, which he typically shied away from. Nor old age looking back, one of his most common endings. It was still wrapped up in the joy of living:

> *I sailed some years upon the seven seas,*
> *One fine day while reachin' on a breeze.*
> *Saw something big way up ahead,* (dramatic pause)
> *School o' whales just a-gettin' out of bed.*

The last couplet didn't work, nor could he find one he liked in the three pages of notes and scratchings. But when he played it through, the full circle came out and had Vonda scrabbling to take the notebook back and write it down.

> *They seemed so free and full of joy,*
> *Reminded me of that little-bitty boy!*

Full circle. It wasn't big, deep, or important. It was pure fluff, but rife with emotion, the emotion of joy from a life spent sailing.

He looked up at Vonda, "You're hired."

Her smile was radiant.

8

VONDA FELT AS IF SHE'D BEEN DRUGGED WITH FAR MORE than a turkey sandwich on fresh-baked sourdough and too much sugar in her iced tea.

She hadn't dared sing along, of course.

Couldn't believe she'd handed over the verses at all. But she hadn't been thinking as she'd scribed and rearranged what Myles had spilled out so effortlessly. Then he'd asked for his own words so she'd handed her notes over before she could stop herself.

It was like Woodie Guthrie, one of the greatest folk singers of all time. He'd spent his entire life spinning out tunes. Hundreds had been collected, but thousands more had probably been played once and lost in the winds atop a train or in front of a campfire as he hoboed around the country for so much of his life. They might *all* have been lost if Alan Lomax hadn't discovered him and recorded so many of them.

Myles would have been willing to let his words spill out over the ocean and be lost.

Yet he'd so captured how she was feeling.

Last night, when she'd called home, Mom had been all worried. Dad had simply said, *Sounds like fun, honey. Do it.*

And here she was on the first day of her first big sailing adventure—and there was a song about it. That was crazy, wild, and wonderful.

The next few days were wet, not stormy, but the rain was steady enough that there was no music on deck.

Rose and Myles had slowly trained her to handle the big wheel, and then the sails. The autopilot did the work most of the time, but they turned it off to teach her. Even with the autopilot, she never stood a watch alone, but she was helping.

Not *being* helped, instead helping.

And the power of steering the big boat was a visceral thrill as if her heart had come alive for the first time in a year.

"You're getting the hang of it," Rose said. It was the six-to-midnight watch. The rain had been left behind and the first stars were peeking through holes in the clouds, seeing if it was safe to come out.

"Thanks." Vonda could be casual around Rose. Myles was still up on a pedestal: musical, funny, handsome, and kind. All except one thing, "Can I ask a personal question?"

And there it lay like a dead fish on the deck with no way for her to pretend she wasn't the one who'd tossed it there.

Rose shrugged a yes, only visible in the darkness

because of the phosphorescent wake their passage was churning up in the ocean.

"Don't you two get along? I mean you're not breaking up, are you?" It came out as a whisper in the night. She could feel Myles sleeping in his bed directly below where they both sat in the cockpit, only feet away.

She could feel Rose's attention but couldn't see her expression or read her silence.

"I mean, you looked so close when I saw you play that night. And you look like an incredible couple from the outside. But you sleep apart. I haven't even seen you touch except to steady each other. I—" Vonda finally managed to get control of her mouth. But it was so wrong.

It's not what she'd been dreaming of when she'd gotten engaged to Greg. It was what she'd feared would never be for her as she lost hair, energy, and the will to do more than survive.

Rose let the night be her answer for a long time before speaking. "Twins."

"What about twins?"

"Us. Myles and me. We're twins. Eleven minutes apart."

Vonda wondered if Rose could see how wide her eyes were. "You... But... No, I saw you two play together. How you were together. How..."

Again, Rose's silence seemed to fill the night for a long while before she spoke. "We've always been really close, twins after all. Whole family is. The music maybe makes that closer because we both love it so much. And when we perform, we've found it useful to let people think we're a couple. Keeps the assertive groupies at bay.

We used to play the field after each gig, but that gets old fast. Better to let folks assume whatever it is they want to assume while we're on stage. Off stage, out of sight, is when we each find someone to be with."

"And have you found somebody?"

"No." Vonda could hear the wistful sadness. And much later, when Vonda was almost asleep in her seat, lulled by the roll of the waves and the soft green glow fading behind them, "Neither has Myles."

9

MYLES HADN'T WOKEN THE GIRLS FOR THE SIX-A.M. changeover because the sunrise had been too lovely to miss. At the nine-a.m. radio check-in, the next nearest boat was six hours and forty miles behind. *Maybelline* was riding the big rollers of the North Pacific like the champion she was. The autopilot had it down. The nights were growing cooler, it wouldn't be shorts and t-shirt at night much longer.

He tiptoed down to fetch his guitar and plugged in a set of headphones. Because he was fingerpicking, the strings were quieter than the creak of the sails. He wouldn't disturb anyone.

Playing through the sailing song, it was impossible not to smile at the morning because it was such a cheery tune. Something was missing, though he wasn't sure quite what. It wasn't Rose's bass line and her rich alto harmony; he could hear those as clearly in his head as if it was his own voice. There was…something more. But try as he could, it eluded him.

Do something else and maybe it would come to him.

He fooled around with some chords, found a pleasant rhythm. It was more ballad and less dance. Their money was in the dance music, but out here in the middle of the ocean, who cared.

> *You never believe it could happen to you,*
> *I don't believe it could happen to me.*
> *Just got together, can't you see?*
> *Two of us just walking along.*

Again the chords were ridiculously simple, but they fit the song.

He tinkered together a couple of verses, but it was the refrain that kept shifting. Not that the first chorus was wrong, but that the chorus evolved, revealing the emotions, as the verses told the surface story. The changing refrain that he'd discovered with the mystery dancer at The Dirty Monkey.

> *Two of us just sailing along.*
> (as the ride smoothed out)
>
> ...
> *Two of us just livin' along.*
> (as a relationship became a life)
>
> ...
> *Two of us just lovin' along*
> (that clear soprano he'd been missing before sounded clear on the morning air and—)

"Whoa!" He snapped back into the moment, realized

he'd been singing aloud, and stared at Vonda sitting across the cockpit from him with her notepad in her hand. "Do that again."

"I—" she blushed fiercely. "Sorry, I didn't mean to." She clenched the notepad in her fist, dropped her pen, reached for it, left it, and scrambled for the ladder to go below.

"No. Wait!"

"What's up?" Rose was half up the ladder, still blinking with sleep.

Vonda, with her escape blocked, turned at bay.

Myles started the chorus again.

He watched Vonda as she stared down at the deck, her jaw clenched. Her grace and balance were shot. He could see that her knees were locked as tightly as her fists but he didn't understand why.

He tried nudging her pen toward her.

She didn't bend down to reach for it. It rolled back and forth with the boat's motion until it bumped against her toe. *That* jolted her to life as if she'd been electrocuted.

She scooped it up, then stumbled on the next wave and crash landed on one of the cockpit seats. Pushing herself upright, she closed her notepad, fruitlessly trying to flatten out the pages she'd crumpled, but still she didn't sing.

Rose had been nodding her head to the tune. She took a deep breath, and opened her mouth.

Myles stopped her joining in with the least shake of his head, and began to repeat the chorus. Still playing the chords that no one but he could hear.

Without looking up, Vonda joined in the second line so softly that it was a whisper barely louder than the wind. By the third line, he could hear her clearly, by the last she was up to perhaps half the volume it should be sung.

It didn't matter. She didn't offer some high harmony. Nor did she echo his melody. As if she too could hear where Rose's voice and bass would slide in seamlessly, she left everything else behind and stitched the two together into a whole.

A countermelody? More of a riff that wandered so far away from the core that it almost sounded wrong until it came back twice as strong when it rejoined his melodic line.

He tried running the refrain again, but this time she kept her silence without looking up.

The chords came to a jangling end over his headphone.

"What did you—"

"Myles," Rose cut him off as she came out on deck. "Why don't you make us some breakfast?"

"But she," he pointed to Vonda though he didn't know *but she* what.

Rose gave him her stop-being-an-idiot eyebrow raise.

Not knowing what else to do, he headed below.

10

This morning Vonda felt none of the peace of sitting in the cockpit with Rose that had so filled last night. She wore cutoffs and a loose shirt that hid her shape and kept the bulk of the sun off her fair skin. SPF50 took care of the rest. But it didn't block all of the nerves inside.

She could feel Rose waiting for her to speak first. As if Vonda had any idea what to say. Maybe tossing herself over the side *wasn't* the worst option.

What was the harm in singing? Yet she'd sung with professional musicians who were completely out of her league. And to take Myles' music and play with it? *Change* it. Yet he hadn't been upset. Instead she'd had the closest thing to a panic attack since...she was twelve?

"I'm the most ridiculous person on the planet!"

Rose did her quiet thing a while longer before asking, "When was the last time you sang?"

"About five minutes ago. Last time *ever!*"

"Um-hmm." Rose did something with the mainsail that Vonda was fairly sure was wholly unnecessary.

"Forever ago. College *a cappella.*" Vonda had enjoyed that. Unaccompanied singing in a group required immaculate tone and immense creativity. They'd been good, too. Did a couple of intercollegiate competitions and ended up near the top.

Rose re-coiled the line she'd displaced but didn't look up as she spoke. "You know that Myles spent three straight days looking for you. Of course, he still hasn't figured out it was you."

"He did? Wait! That *what* was me?"

"I think you're a *who* not a *what* but I'm just guessing."

"Rose!"

Rose finally looked at her and smiled. She'd burned away Vonda's nerves by ticking her off.

"That *who* was me?"

Through the hatch from below Myles began handing out breakfast: mugs of coffee in steel to-go cups, orange juice in sippy bottles that wouldn't spill, and bowls of yogurt with Grape Nuts, fresh fruit, and a drizzle of honey. All that healthy fiber she was supposed to eat regularly and so rarely did.

He finally joined them.

Rose was keeping a half smile to herself—mostly. Vonda was slowly learning that Rose might be quiet, but she was sneaky. Myles reminded her of the golden retriever they'd had when she was a kid, fun and always eager—but not nearly so deep a thinker.

Vonda concentrated on her breakfast.

"Myles," Rose said so casually that Vonda went on instant alert. Was it too late to go eat in her cabin? "Why don't you tell Vonda about your mystery dancer?"

"Mystery dancer?" And Vonda knew she'd put her foot in it. Now she'd have to stay.

As he began telling the story of their first night at The Dirty Monkey, Rose's smile grew. Part of it was clearly at some joke Vonda didn't understand, yet. But most of it was love for her brother. She could see that now. Being twins explained so much of the dynamic between them. They were so...

Myles began talking about the mystery dancer —*Mystery Dancer* Rose mouthed at her without interrupting her brother—who had appeared early in the second set.

"Always at the back of the crowd. Hard to see. With this long Hawaiian scarf covering her hair. But my God the way she danced."

The more he explained, the more Vonda suspected.

Her?

It was impossible. Myles wasn't describing her physicality, her out-of-shape body, the betrayal of her breasts producing a cancer that had shattered the life she'd known. He was describing her like...music.

Definitely her.

"I, we," he nodded to include Rose, "have never played like that before. Or since. It was like an ocean I'd never sailed before, and now never can again. I searched for her, but she never came back."

"Are you sure you'd recognize her when she does?" Rose winked at Vonda.

"How could I miss her? An angel of music. She could croak like a frog and still be a muse. She made the music do things I can't find again."

"It's only been a few days."

"Nine days. Nine days and eleven goddamn hours from the end of that last set to now!" It was the first time she'd heard words of anger from either of the twins. He looked at his watch. "And fourteen minutes!" he practically spit it out.

Vonda shook her head.

No! Rose *thought* it had been her but, even if she was right, she was still wrong. It was impossible. Vonda knew she was a broken thing, not some magic talisman that Myles wished to worship from afar.

Vonda collected their empty bowls and carried them below to wash.

She avoided the sadness in both of their eyes: Myles at his loss and Rose at Vonda's cowardice.

11

"ARE YOU OKAY?" MYLES KEPT HIS VOICE LOW.

All yesterday and last night there'd been no sign of Vonda. And Rose hadn't said an unneeded word, which with the unusually fine sailing weather had been few and far between.

Vonda looked...haunted when she emerged into the morning sunlight. He searched her face for the joy that had been there the day she'd boarded the boat, but it had been wiped away.

She shook her head no. "But hiding isn't fixing anything." She eased onto the seat on the other side of the big wheel he sat behind. It was like she was cut up into pieces by the spokes. She looked so upset that he moved from the helmsman's seat to sit across from her in front of the wheel.

The wind was unusually steady, no storm nor any expected. *Maybelline* was managing well on the new heading Rose had tacked to last night. They had altered course from due north to northeast as the North Pacific

Gyre turned to join the Japanese current. If this held, they could maybe even fly the spinnaker, though even with three that would be a challenge. Definitely not two with their level of experience.

"Is it something I said?"

Again she shook head, but then she offered an uncertain shrug.

"We can double back. It'll be a rougher ride against the wind, but *Vapor* is only fifteen hours behind us. I'm sure they have room if you want to change boats."

She shook her head again; no follow-up shrug this time.

"Do you want me to get Rose? She's worried about you." Or maybe pissed at him, but when he'd asked, she'd simply said, *Your watch,* then gone below. "I guess I am too."

"I…" Vonda's voice cracked from lack of use, then she swore so violently that he laughed. "I'm so *sick* of being frail."

"Then don't be."

She looked up at him. Her light brown eyes studying his face. "It's not that easy."

"Sure it is. There's the past, the present, and the future. Which do you want to live in?"

"Myles," it was the first time she'd used his name and he liked the way it sounded. "The past has consequences."

"Does it?"

When she started to protest, he rested a hand on hers to stop her. It was the first time they'd touched. Her hands weren't frail, they were delicate.

"I'm not being facetious. So many great songwriters have covered this ground. Kathy Matea, *You've Got to Dance.*"

"Yeah, sure. Tim McGraw, *Live Like You Were Dying.* Been there. Done that." She looked even sadder which shouldn't be possible.

He wanted to grab his guitar and play a song for her but a tune about the joys of sailing didn't seem on the mark at the moment. He knew his own shortcomings.

"Look, Vonda, I'm crap at expressing myself except through music. Half the time I don't even hear..." And then her words sunk in.

"*Been there? Done that?*"

She seemed to cower, but nodded.

"Are you okay now?"

"Except for the lifetime threat of relapse, *sure.*" Then she slapped her hand across her mouth and almost darted down the ladder once more.

He kept his hand on hers to keep her in place. "I can't imagine how hard that must be."

"It's..." her voice choked behind her hand, "...not easy."

Unsure what else to do, he shifted to sit beside her and went to pat her on the back. Surprisingly, she turned into his shoulder and burst into tears.

It only took seconds before Rose was halfway up the ladder and glaring at him.

What's happening, he mouthed to her.

Rose froze in position, listening to Vonda's weeping, then nodded to herself. She descended the stairs again and he heard her room's door close. That was crazy.

Unable to move, he stroked Vonda's short hair, fluffy and softer than any he'd ever touched before. Then he ran his hand down her back in what he hoped was a soothing gesture.

For a mile or more, the only sound on board was the slap of lines and Vonda's quiet sniffles. He looked for something to distract himself from how nice she felt in his arms. Sun was up in the sky. A few clouds too small to portend anything, just going about their own business. The rollers wide and deep rocked the boat gently. Not a bird around. He didn't see them much this far out, unless there was a big school of fish for them to feast on. He could even hear the tiny hum of the autopilot as its motors whirred on and off to maintain their heading.

Finally Vonda sniffled to herself and apologized quietly.

"No problem. I'm always at a loss about what to do with a weeping woman. This is nothing new."

"A lot of practice?" she managed on a choked voice.

"Not a lot, but some."

She patted his shoulder. "You do just fine, Myles."

"Something you want to talk about?"

Vonda shook her head. "But I guess you earned the right to know."

His emotions went through a thousand changes as she told him the story of her illness. Shock, pity, blind fury at her asshole fiancé's dumping her, and all the rest of it.

"And you call yourself frail? I hope I'm half as strong if anything like that ever comes my way. You are sailing thousands of miles across the open ocean. You know how few people would dare do that, never mind actually try? Right there, you're a rare breed."

"You aren't repulsed?"

"Why would I be?"

Vonda studied him from so close he could see the patterns of her irises. "Or pitying me?"

"Feeling sorry for you, sure. That was a rough storm to ride through. But it makes me think more rather than less of you for coming through that with so much joy."

"Joy?" she gasped in disbelief.

He sang,

First time I ever sailed a boat...

She threw her head back and laughed like a release. She joined him on the chorus. Somewhere in the second verse, Rose came on deck with their bass and guitar and soon the three of them were singing together.

They repeated the chorus several times, each building on the one before. Vonda's voice soon soared above theirs in flights of purest fancy.

And his fingers shifted. Not changing the chords, but augmenting them. Adding notes from his low E-string when Rose climbed up from her bass' high-G. Finding flourishes to tease Vonda's high notes that sent her spinning off into—

His fingers jangled on the strings.

"Holy shit!" He turned to Vonda. "I've been looking everywhere for you!"

12

Vonda cringed. She'd forgotten herself and let Myles' kindness sweep her away. It had felt so good to let the music unleash all of the pain she hadn't been able to show in front of her parents. A year's pain and fear had spilled out of her—and turned to joy.

That was the miracle.

That, and Myles hadn't walked away.

Instead, he'd held her hand and told her how amazingly strong she was.

That wasn't any version of herself she recognized.

Myles turned to Rose but pointed his finger at Vonda, "She'd MD." Then he turned to face her. "You're MD."

"No, I'm V, Vonda Decosta."

"No you aren't. You're the woman who made the music with her body. Seriously, I spent three straight days driving Rose crazy as I combed Lahaina looking for you."

"And now that you found me?" She held up her chin. She wasn't merely some phantom.

He'd driven her to go and hide in her cabin because

he'd painted a picture of a living miracle that she could never live up to. She'd had Myles on a pedestal, still did. But he'd had her standing atop a skyscraper.

And yet...he didn't.

She'd lost her shit and spilled her life all over the cockpit.

His response was fury at Greg—and telling her how amazing she was.

"Now that I found you?" Myles laughed. "First, you're going to get out that damn notebook of yours."

"And then?"

He kissed her on the nose. "And then, who knows!"

13

Vonda stood on the edge of the stage at Q Nightclub. The place was packed. She managed a wave to Mom and Dad, seated on the edge of the dance floor but not for long. She knew Mom would drag Dad onto the floor soon enough.

Three months after coming ashore to work on their act and attract the attention of the bigger clubs. What would three more months bring?

"Tonight, at the Q," an announcer called out, "we're proud to present VMR, the Vic-Maui Return Band."

The three of them had agreed that the band's name had two meanings. The public one and the private one just for them: Vonda, Myles, and Rose.

Rose lay down a heavy bass beat that caught everyone's attention. It was the irresistible pulse of the sea. Sure enough, Mom was already rising to her feet.

Vonda felt her knee flex with the rhythm to keep her balance, as would be necessary on a sailboat slipping over the waves.

Myles slid in with a happy pulse of dolphins.

The beat was building through her body as Myles and Rose built the ocean through which the song would swim.

The crowd was shifting from the bar and tables to the dance floor. Soon the place was hopping.

Vonda felt the full song.

She felt the music they'd built during their four remaining weeks on the sea. The beauty of starry skies and brilliant sunrises. The agony of fear turned to ecstasy by the first time she and Myles had made love. They'd skipped over dating and sex and moved straight into the purest joy she'd ever found.

She glanced at Rose so lost in the music that her eyes had slid shut.

Maybe they'd find a fourth initial someday. Someone for her future sister-in-law.

For now, Vonda gave herself to the music.

Her eyes were wide open. She saw the journey so clearly. Not the one downwards that had come so close to finishing her. Her imagination and her heart were caught in the upwards one ahead that was so rich with promise.

She'd have to suggest the idea to Myles, he was their master composer. He built, Rose embellished, and Vonda brought the wind to fill the sails.

She lifted her mike to her mouth and let the joy race ahead.

———

If you enjoyed this story
please consider leaving a review.
They really help

Keep reading for an exciting excerpt from:
Where Dreams #1: *Where Dreams are Born*

WHERE DREAMS ARE BORN (EXCERPT)

IF YOU ENJOYED THAT, YOU'LL LOVE THIS TALE!

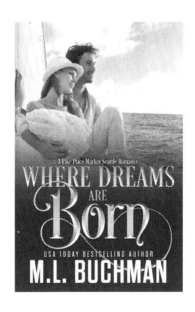

WHERE DREAMS ARE BORN
(EXCERPT)

Russell leaned his back against the studio door after he locked it behind the last of the staff. He barely managed the energy to turn off his camera.

He knew it was good. The images were there; he'd really captured them.

But something was missing.

The groove ran so clean when he slid into it. First his Manhattan high-ceilinged loft would fade into the background, then the strobe lights, reflector umbrellas, and green-screen backdrops all became texture and tone.

Image, camera, and man then became one and nothing else mattered—a single flow of light, beginning before time was counted, and ending its journey in the printed image. One ray of primordial light traveling forever to glisten off the BMW roadster still parked in one corner of the rough-planked wood floor worn smooth by generations of use. Another ray lost in the dark blackness of the finest leather bucket seats. A hundred more picking out the supermodel's perfect hand dangling a single shining and golden key—the image shot just slow enough that the key blurred as it spun, but the logo remained clear.

He couldn't quite put his finger on it...

It would be another great ad by Russell Morgan, Inc. The client would be knocked dead—the ad leaving all others standing still as it roared down the passing lane. This one might get him another Clio, or even a second Mobius.

But...

There wasn't usually a "but."

And there definitely wasn't supposed to be one.

The groove had definitely been there, but he hadn't been in it.

That was the problem. It had slid along, sweeping his staff into their own orchestrated perfection, but he'd remained untouched. That ideal, seamless flow hadn't included him at all.

"Be honest, boyo, that session sucked," he told the empty studio. Everything had come together so perfectly for yet another ad for yet another high-end glossy. *Man, the Magazine* would launch spectacularly in a few weeks, a high-profile mid-December launch, and it would include a never before seen twelve-page spread by the great Russell Morgan. The rag would probably never pay off the lavish launch party of hope, ice sculptures, and chilled magnums of champagne before disappearing like a thousand before it.

"Morose much?"

The studio kept its thoughts to itself—the first reliable sign that he wasn't totally losing his shit.

He stowed the last camera with the others piled by his computer. At the breaker box he shut off the umbrellas, spots, scoops, and washes. The studio shifted from a stark landscape in hard-edged relief to a nest of curious shadows and rounded forms. The tang of hot metal and deodorant were the only lasting result of the day's efforts.

"Get your shit together, Russell." His reflection in the darkened window, stories above the streetlights of West 10th, was unimpressed and proved it was wise enough to not answer back. There was never a "down" after a shoot; there was always an "up."

Not tonight.

He'd kept everyone late—even though it was Thanksgiving eve—hoping for that smooth slide of image-camera-man. It was only when he saw the power of the images he captured that he knew he wasn't a part of the chain anymore and decided he'd paid enough triple-time expenses.

The next to last two-page spread would be the killer —shot with the door open against a background as black as the sports car's finish, the model's single perfect leg wrapped in thigh-high red-leather boots all that was visible in the driver's seat. The sensual juxtaposition of woman and sleek machine served as an irresistible focus. It was an ad designed to wrap every person with even a hint of a Y-chromosome around its little finger. And those with only X-chromosomes would simply want to be her. He'd shot a perfect combo of sex for the guys and power for the women.

Even the final one-page image, a close-up of driver's seat from exactly the same angle, revealing not the model but instead a single rose of precisely the same hue as the leather boot, hadn't moved him despite its perfection.

Without him noticing, Russell had become no more than the observer, merely a technician behind the camera. Now that he faced it, months, maybe even a year had passed since he'd been yanked all the way into the light-image-camera-man slipstream. Tonight was a wakeup call and he didn't like it one bit. Wakeup calls happened to others, not him. But tonight he could no longer ignore it, he hadn't even trailed along in the churned-up wake.

"You're just a creative cog in the advertising machine." Ouch! That one stung, but it didn't turn aside the relentless steamroller of his thoughts speeding down some empty, godforsaken autobahn.

His career was roaring ahead, his business' growth running fast and smooth. But, now that he considered it, he really didn't give a damn.

His life looked perfect, but—"Don't think it!"—his autobahn mind finished despite the command, *it wasn't.*

Russell left his silent reflection to its own thoughts and went through the back door that led to his apartment —closing it tightly on the perfect BMW, the perfect rose, and somewhere, lost among a hundred other props from dozens of other shoots, the long pair of perfect red-leather Chanel boots that had been wrapped around the most expensive legs in Manhattan. He didn't care if he never walked back through that door again. He'd been doing his art by rote; how god-awful sad was that?

And just to rub salt in the wound, he shot *commercial* art.

He'd never had the patience to do art for art's sake. Delayed gratification was his idea of no fun at all. He left the apartment dark with only the city's soft glow through the blind-covered windows revealing the vaguest outlines of the framed art on the wall. Even that almost overwhelmed him tonight.

He didn't want to see the huge prints by the *art* artists: autographed Goldsworthy, Liebowitz, and Joseph Francis' photomosaics for the moderns. A hundred and fifty rare, even one-of-a-kind prints adorned his walls—all the way back through Bourke-White to Russell's prize, an original Daguerre. The Museum of Modern Art kept begging to borrow his collection for a show...and at the moment he was half tempted to dump the whole lot in their Dumpster if they didn't want it.

Crossing the one-room loft apartment—as spacious as the studio—he bypassed the circle of avant-garde chairs that were almost as uncomfortable as they looked and avoided the lush black-leather wrap-around sectional sofa of such ludicrous scale that it could be a playpen for two or host a party for twenty. He cracked the fridge in the stainless-steel-and-black corner kitchen searching for something other than his usual beer.

A bottle of Krug.

Maybe he was just being grouchy after a long day's work.

Juice.

No. He'd run his enthusiasm into the ground but good.

Milk even.

Would he miss the camera if he never picked it up again?

No reaction.

Nothing.

Not even an itch in his palm.

That was an emptiness he did not want to face. Especially not alone, in his apartment, in the middle of the world's most vibrant city.

Russell turned away, and just as the door swung closed, the last sliver of light—the relentless chilly blue-white of the refrigerator bulb—shone across his bed. A quick grab snagged the edge of the door and left the narrow beam illuminating a long pale form on his black-silk bedspread.

The Chanel boots weren't in the studio after all. They were still wrapped around those three thousand dollar-an-hour legs: the only clothing on a perfect body. Five foot-eleven of intensely toned female anatomy right down to an exquisitely stair-mastered behind. Her long, white-blonde hair lay as a perfect Godiva over her tanned breasts—except for their too exact symmetry, even the closest inspection didn't reveal the work done there. She lay with one leg raised just ever so slightly to hide what was meant to be revealed later.

Melanie.

By the steady rise and fall of her flat stomach, he knew she'd fallen asleep while waiting for him to finish in the studio.

How long had they been an item? Two months? Three?

She'd made him feel alive...at least when he was

actually with her. Melanie was the super-model in his bed or on his arm at yet another SoHo gallery opening. Together they journeyed to sharp parties and trendy three-star restaurants where she dazzled and wooed yet another gathering of New York's finest with her ever so soft, so sensual, and so studied French accent. Together they were wired into the heart of the in-crowd.

But that wasn't him, was it? It didn't sound like the Russell he once knew.

Perhaps "they" were about how *he* looked on *her* arm?

Did she know tomorrow was the annual Thanksgiving ordeal at his parents? The grand holiday gathering that he'd rather die than attend? Any number of eligible woman would be floating about his parents' house out in Greenwich; anyone able to finagle an invitation would attend in hopes of snaring one of *People Magazine's* "100 Most Eligible." They all wanted to land the heir to a billion or some such; though he was wealthy enough on his own, by his own sweat, to draw anyone's attention. He ranked number twenty-four on the list this year—up from forty-seven the year before despite Tom Cruise being available yet again.

But not Melanie. He knew that it wasn't the money that drew her. Yes, she wanted him. But even more, she wanted the life that came with him—wrapped in the man-package. She wanted The Life. The one that *People Magazine* readers dreamed about between glossy pages.

His fingertips were growing cold where they held the refrigerator door cracked open.

If he woke her there'd be amazing sex. Or a great party to go to. Or...

Did he want "Or"? What more did he want from her?

Sex. Companionship. An energy, a vivacity, a thirst he feared that he lacked. Yes.

But where was that smooth synchronicity hiding, like the light-image-camera-man of photography that he'd lost? Where lurked that perfect flow from one person to another? Did she feel it? Could he ever feel it? Did it even exist?

"More?" he whispered into the darkness to test the sound. He knew all about wanting more.

The refrigerator door slid shut—escaping from his numbed fingers—which plunged the apartment back into darkness, taking Melanie along with it.

His breath echoed in the vast darkness. Proof that he was alive if nothing more.

It was time to close the studio—time to be done with Russell Incorporated.

Then what?

Maybe Angelo would know what to do. He always claimed that he did. Maybe this time Russell would actually listen to his almost-brother, though he knew from the experience of being himself for the last thirty years that was unlikely.

Seattle.

Damn! He'd have to go to bloody Seattle to find his best friend. There was a possible upside to such a trip— maybe there'd be a flight out before tomorrow's mess at his parents'. He slapped his pocket, but once again he'd set his phone down in some unknown corner of the studio and it would take forever to find. He really needed two—one chained down so that he could always find it to call the other.

Russell considered the darkness. He could guarantee that Seattle wouldn't be a big hit with Melanie.

Now if he only knew whether that was a good thing or bad.

———

Keep reading now!
A great tale of romance and adventure,
Of sailboats, food, fashion, and fun.
Available at fine retailers everywhere.
Where Dreams are Born

And please don't forget that review for Solo Passage.

ABOUT THE AUTHOR

USA Today and Amazon #1 Bestseller M. L. "Matt" Buchman has 70+ action-adventure thriller and military romance novels, 100 short stories, and lotsa audiobooks. PW says: "Tom Clancy fans open to a strong female lead will clamor for more." Booklist declared: "3X Top 10 of the Year." A project manager with a geophysics degree, he's designed and built houses, flown and jumped out of planes, solo-sailed a 50' sailboat, and bicycled solo around the world...and he quilts. More at: www. mlbuchman.com.

Other works by M. L. Buchman: (* - also in audio)

Action-Adventure Thrillers

Dead Chef
One Chef!
Two Chef!

Miranda Chase
Drone*
Thunderbolt*
Condor*
Ghostrider*
Raider*
Chinook*
Havoc*
White Top*
Start the Chase*

Science Fiction / Fantasy

Deities Anonymous
Cookbook from Hell: Reheated
Saviors 101

Single Titles
Monk's Maze
the Me and Elsie Chronicles

Contemporary Romance

Eagle Cove
Return to Eagle Cove
Recipe for Eagle Cove
Longing for Eagle Cove
Keepsake for Eagle Cove

Love Abroad
Heart of the Cotswolds: England
Path of Love: Cinque Terre, Italy

Where Dreams
Where Dreams are Born
Where Dreams Reside
Where Dreams Are of Christmas*
Where Dreams Unfold
Where Dreams Are Written
Where Dreams Continue

Non-Fiction

Strategies for Success
Managing Your Inner Artist/Writer
Estate Planning for Authors*
Character Voice
Narrate and Record Your Own
Audiobook*

Short Story Series by M. L. Buchman:

Action-Adventure Thrillers

Dead Chef

Miranda Chase Origin Stories

Romantic Suspense

Antarctic Ice Fliers

US Coast Guard

Contemporary Romance

Eagle Cove

Other

Deities Anonymous (fantasy)

Single Titles

The Emily Beale Universe
(military romantic suspense)

The Night Stalkers
MAIN FLIGHT
The Night Is Mine
I Own the Dawn
Wait Until Dark
Take Over at Midnight
Light Up the Night
Bring On the Dusk
By Break of Day
Target of the Heart
Target Lock on Love
Target of Mine
Target of One's Own
NIGHT STALKERS HOLIDAYS
Daniel's Christmas*
Frank's Independence Day*
Peter's Christmas*
Christmas at Steel Beach
Zachary's Christmas*
Roy's Independence Day*
Damien's Christmas*
Christmas at Peleliu Cove

Henderson's Ranch
Nathan's Big Sky*
Big Sky, Loyal Heart*
Big Sky Dog Whisperer*
Tales of Henderson's Ranch*

Shadow Force: Psi
At the Slightest Sound*
At the Quietest Word*
At the Merest Glance*
At the Clearest Sensation*

White House Protection Force
Off the Leash*
On Your Mark*
In the Weeds*

Firehawks
Pure Heat
Full Blaze
Hot Point*
Flash of Fire*
Wild Fire

SMOKEJUMPERS
Wildfire at Dawn*
Wildfire at Larch Creek*
Wildfire on the Skagit*

Delta Force
Target Engaged*
Heart Strike*
Wild Justice*
Midnight Trust*

Emily Beale Universe Short Story Series
The Night Stalkers
The Night Stalkers Stories
The Night Stalkers CSAR
The Night Stalkers Wedding Stories
The Future Night Stalkers

Delta Force
Th Delta Force Shooters
The Delta Force Warriors

Firehawks
The Firehawks Lookouts
The Firehawks Hotshots
The Firebirds

White House Protection Force
Stories

Future Night Stalkers
Stories (Science Fiction)

SIGN UP FOR M. L. BUCIIMAN'S NEWSLETTER TODAY

and receive:
Release News
Free Short Stories
a Free Book

Get your free book today. Do it now.
free-book.mlbuchman.com

Printed in Great Britain
by Amazon